Walker Books is grateful for permission to reproduce the following:

The Monster Stomp from *Game Songs with Prof Dogg's Troupe* is reproduced by kind permission of the writer, John Perry, A & C Black (Publishers) Ltd and Inter-Action Inprint.

Naughty Soap Song by Dorothy Aldis is reprinted by permission of G. P. Putnam's Sons from *All Together* copyright 1925–1928, 1934, 1939, 1952, © renewed 1953–1956, 1962, 1967 by Dorothy Aldis.

Remember by Pamela Mordecai is reproduced by permission of the copyright holder, Ginn and Company Ltd.

Sugarcake Bubble, **Hippity-Hippity-Hatch** and **Tumble Drying** are reproduced with permission of Curtis Brown Group Ltd, London. Copyright © Grace Nichols 1991.

First published 1996 by Walker Books Ltd
87 Vauxhall Walk
London SE11 5HJ

This edition published 2002

2 4 6 8 10 9 7 5 3 1

Text © year of publication individual authors
Illustrations © year of publication individual illustrators
Cover illustrations © Chris Riddell

This book has been typeset in ITC Garamond.

Printed in Italy

British Library Cataloguing in Publication Data:
a catalogue record for this book is
available from the British Library

ISBN 0-7445-8878-2

The
WALKER
TREASURY
of
FIRST
RHYMES

WALKER BOOKS

AND SUBSIDIARIES

LONDON • BOSTON • SYDNEY

CONTENTS

Out and About

by Shirley Hughes

Sand

I like sand.
The run-between-your-fingers kind,
The build-it-into-castles kind.
Mountains of sand meeting the sky,
Flat sand, going on for ever.
I *do* like sand.

Water

I like water.

The shallow,

      splashy,

            paddly kind,

The hold-on-tight-it's-deep kind.

Slosh it out of buckets,
Spray it all around.

I *do* like water.

Wind

I like the wind.
The soft, summery, gentle kind,
The gusty, blustery, fierce kind.
Ballooning out the curtains,
Blowing things about,
Wild and wilful everywhere.
I *do* like the wind.

Mud

I like mud.

The slippy, sloppy, squelchy kind,
     The slap-it-into-pies kind.

     Stir it up in puddles,
          Slither and slide.

          I *do* like mud.

Monkeys on the Bed

illustrated by Chris Riddell

Three little monkeys
Jumping on the bed;
One fell off
And knocked his head.

Momma called the doctor,
The doctor said:
"No more monkeys
Jumping on the bed."

Michael Foreman's

RING-A-RING O' ROSES

Ring-a-ring o' roses,
A pocket full of posies,
  A-tishoo! A-tishoo!
We all fall down.

The cows are in the meadow,
Lying fast asleep,
  A-tishoo! A-tishoo!
We all get up again.

Mother Goose

GOOSE FEATHERS

Cackle, cackle, Mother Goose,
Have you any feathers loose?
Truly have I, pretty fellow,
Half enough to fill a pillow.
Here are quills, take one or two,
And down to make a bed for you.

LITTLE BIRD

Once I saw a little bird
  Come hop, hop, hop;
So I cried, Little bird,
  Will you stop, stop, stop?

I was going to the window
  To say, How do you do?
But he shook his little tail,
  And far away he flew.

JERRY HALL

Jerry Hall
He is so small,
A rat could eat him,
Hat and all.

HERE COME THE
BABIES

by **Catherine** *and* **Laurence Anholt**

What do babies look like?

Wriggles and dribbles and sticking out ears,
Little round faces with rivers of tears.
Babies wear suits which are long at the toes,
They stick out in the middle and up at the nose.

What do babies play with?

Bobbles and bows, fingers and toes,
Shoes and hats, sleeping cats,
Frizzy hair, saggy bear,
Empty box, Daddy's socks.

What do lots of babies do?

One baby bouncing on her brother's knee,
Two in a play-pen, three by the sea,
Four babies yelling while their mummies try to talk,
Five babies, holding hands, learning how to walk.

Yum Yum!

Bread for the ducks,
quack, quack, quack.

Bread for the goose,
stand well back.

Milk for the cat,
lap, lap, lap.

A worm for the bird,
see him flap.

HIPPITY-HIPPITY-HATCH

Hippity-Hippity-Hatch
My black fowl's on her patch
Keeping her eggs
All cosy and warm
Hippity-Hippity-Hatch.

Hippity-Hippity-Hatch
My black fowl's left her patch
Her chicks have all cracked
Into the world
Hippity-Hippity-Hatch.

TUMBLE DRYING

Spin Spin Spin
Tumble tumble tumble
Short and tall
Big and small
All go round and round.

Spin Spin Spin
Tumble tumble tumble
Nylon and cotton
Zip-up and button
All go round and round.

BABY RHYMES

Clap Hands

Clap hands, dance and spin,
Open wide and pop it in,
Blow a trumpet, bang a drum,
Wave to Daddy, wave to Mum.

Tickle, Tickle

Squelch, squelch, in the mud,
Splish, splash, scrub-a-dub,
Gently, gently, brush your hair,
Tickle, tickle, under there.

Helen Oxenbury

All Fall Down

Singing all together,
Running round and round,
Bouncy, bouncy, on the bed,
All fall down.

Say Goodnight

Up, down, up in the sky,
Swing low, swing high,
Bumpetty, bumpetty, hold on tight,
Hush, little babies, say goodnight.

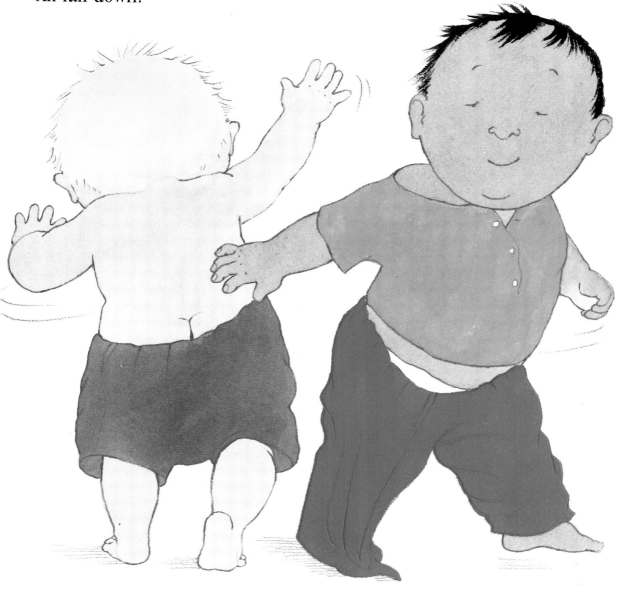

RHYMES FROM OVER THE MOON

illustrated by

Charlotte Voake

Humpty Dumpty
Sat on a wall,
Humpty Dumpty
Had a great fall.

All the King's horses
And all the King's men
Couldn't put Humpty
together again.

The man in the wilderness asked me,
How many strawberries grow in the sea?
I answered him, as I thought good,
As many as red herrings
grow in the wood.

I had a little nut tree,
  Nothing would it bear
But a silver nutmeg
  And a golden pear.
The king of Spain's daughter
  Came to visit me,
And all for the sake
  Of my little nut tree.
I skipped over water,
  I danced over sea,
And all the birds in the air
  Couldn't catch me.

Goosey, goosey gander,
Who stands yonder?
Little Betty Baker.
Take her up and shake her.

Pat-a-cake, pat-a-cake, baker's man,
Bake me a cake as fast as you can.
Pat it and prick it, and mark it with T,
Put it in the oven for Tommy and me.

THIS IS THE
BEAR

by **Sarah Hayes**   *illustrated by* **Helen Craig**

This is the bear who fell in the bin.
This is the dog who pushed him in.

This is the man who picked up the sack.
This is the driver who would not come back.

This is the bear who went to the dump
and fell on the pile with a bit of a bump.

This is the boy who took the bus
and went to the dump to make a fuss.

This is the man in an awful grump
who searched and searched and searched the dump.

This is the bear all cold and cross
who did not think he was really lost.

This is the dog who smelled the smell
of a bone and a tin and a bear as well.

This is the man who drove them home –
the boy, the bear and the dog with a bone.

This is the bear all lovely and clean
who did not say just where he had been.

This is the boy who knew quite well,
but promised his friend he would not tell.

And this is the boy
who woke up in the night

and asked the bear
if he felt all right –

and was very surprised
when the bear shouted out,

"How soon can we have
another day out?"

31

TWO CARIBBEAN POEMS

REMEMBER

Remember when
the world was tall
and you were small
and legs were all
you saw?

Thin legs
fat legs
dog legs
cat legs.

Table legs
chair legs
dark legs
fair legs.

Quick legs
slow legs
nowhere-
to-go legs.

Jumping legs
prancing legs
skipping legs
dancing legs.

Shoes-and-sock legs
on the rocks legs.

Standing-very-tall legs
running-all-around legs.

Stooping-very-small legs
lying-on-the-ground legs.

Remember when
the world was tall
and you were small
and legs were all
you saw?

Pamela Mordecai

32

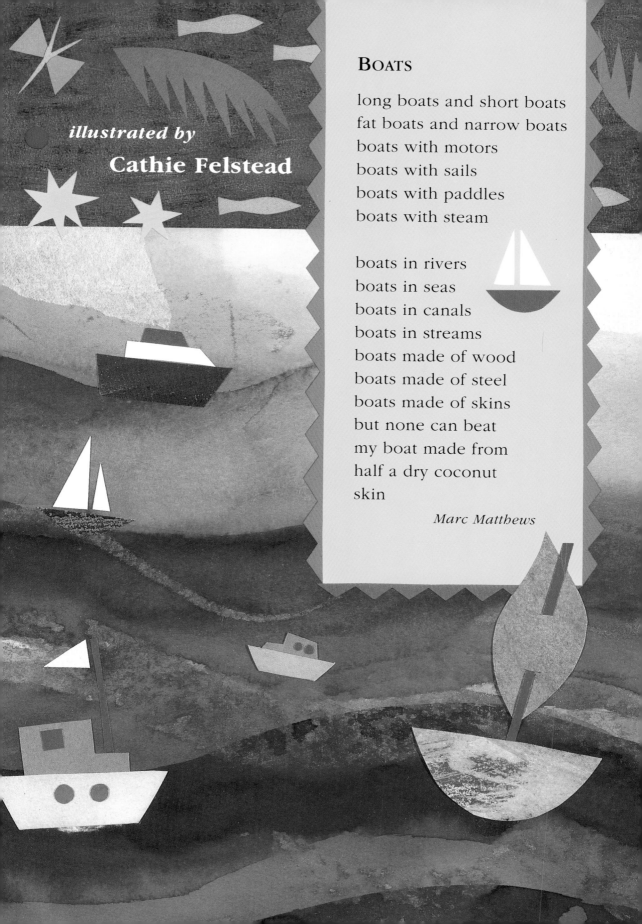

illustrated by
Cathie Felstead

BOATS

long boats and short boats
fat boats and narrow boats
boats with motors
boats with sails
boats with paddles
boats with steam

boats in rivers
boats in seas
boats in canals
boats in streams
boats made of wood
boats made of steel
boats made of skins
but none can beat
my boat made from
half a dry coconut
skin

Marc Matthews

The Train Ride

by **June Crebbin**

illustrated by
Stephen Lambert

We're off on a journey
Out of the town –
What shall I see?
What shall I see?

Sheep running off
And cows lying down,
That's what I see,
That's what I see.

Over the meadow,
Up on the hill,
What shall I see?
What shall I see?

A mare and her foal
Standing perfectly still,
That's what I see,
That's what I see.

There is a farm
Down a bumpety road –
What shall I see?
What shall I see?

A shiny red tractor
Pulling its load,
That's what I see,
That's what I see.

So trok with the frullops
and chase every sun.
Yoop dooz, little Grog.
Let's have fun!
Let's have fun!

GOOD ZAP
Good zap, little Grog,
the moons have turned pink.
The giant chiwangas
are starting to sink.

In the dusk of the garden
a wild fribbet humms,
and all the blue zamblots
are covered in flumms.

So wave to the smuffits
and bring in your grib.
In your soft, furry nightclothes,
bounce into your crib.

Now dream with the froozels
and snuggle your feet.
Good zap, little Grog.
Go to sleep.
Go to sleep.

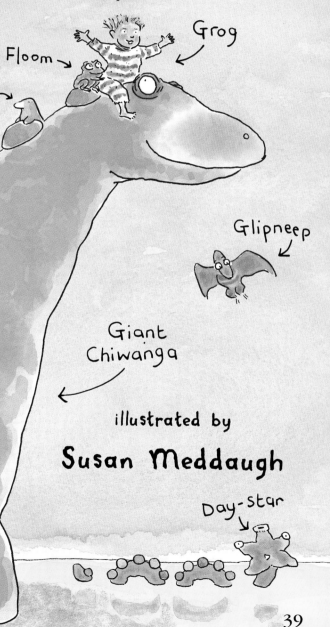

Zibblet →

Floom →

Grog ←

Smuffit →

Zamblot ↓

Wild fribbet ↓

Froozel ↓

Glipneep ↓

Giant Chiwanga ←

illustrated by

Susan Meddaugh

Day-star ↓

Down at the Doctor's

Down at the doctor's
where everybody goes
there's a fat white cat
with a dribbly bibbly nose,
with a dribble dribble here
and a bibble bibble there,
that's the way
she dribbles her nose.

Down at the doctor's
where everybody goes
there's a fat black dog
with messy missy toes,
    with a mess mess here
    and a miss miss there,
    that's the way
    she messes her toes.

Down at the doctor's
    where everybody goes
    there's a fat red parrot
    who everybody knows,
    with a hi-de-hi here
    and a how-de-how there,
    that's the parrot
    that everybody knows.

Messing Around

"Do you know what?"
said Jumping John.
"I had a belly ache
and now it's gone."

"Do you know what?"
said Kicking Kirsty.
"All this jumping
has made me thirsty."

"Do you know what?"
said Mad Mickey.
"I sat in some glue
and I feel all sticky."

"Do you know what?"
said Fat Fred.
"You can't see me,
I'm under the bed."

Michael Rosen   *illustrated by* **Quentin Blake**

A
CUP OF

STARSHINE

illustrated by
Graham Percy

OH, JEMIMA

Oh, Jemima,
Look at your Uncle Jim!
He's down in the duckpond
Learning how to swim.
First he's on his
Left leg,
Then he's on his
Right –

Now he's on a bar of soap,
Skidding out of
Sight!

I scream,
    You scream
    We all scream
    For ice-cream.

Mother
    made a
        seedy
            cake –

        Gave us
        all the
    belly
ache.

Big fat
juicy ones,

Little squiggly
niggly ones.

Going in
the garden

To eat
worms.

Caveman Dave and

Caveman Dave
lives in a cave,
he doesn't wash
and doesn't shave.
He's smelly
but he's very brave.

Wild animals
don't frighten Dave,
at bears and tigers
he will wave.
Dave really is
extremely brave –

but Dave's sister
Ava is braver!

Mrs Pirate

by Nick Sharratt

When Mrs Pirate went shopping
she bought an apple pie
and a patch for her eye,
a bar of soap
and a telescope,
an onion and a carrot
and a red and green parrot,
some knickers and a vest
and an old treasure chest,
buttons for her coat
and a big sailing boat,
a packet of tea
and some sea.

MOON FROG

by *Richard Edwards*
 illustrated by *Sarah Fox-Davies*

The moon slid down the sky,
The froggy whispered, "Soon,
If only it comes close enough,
I'll leap on to the moon."

The moon slid lower still,
The froggy paused, then – hop!
His long legs launched him at the moon
And landed him on top.

The moon sailed smoothly on
Along its starry course,
With froggy proudly riding
Like a jockey on a horse.

IF I HAD A
MONSTER

by Colin McNaughton

If I had a monster,
I'll tell you what I'd do:
I'd starve it for a week
And then I'd set it on you!

I never saw a purple cow

and other nonsense rhymes

THE PURPLE COW

I never saw a purple cow,
I never hope to see one;
But I can tell you, anyhow,
I'd rather see than be one.

illustrated by Emma Chichester Clark

THERE WAS A PIG

There was a Pig, that sat alone,
   Beside a ruined pump.
By day and night he made his moan:
It would have stirred a heart of stone
   To see him wring his hoofs and groan,
Because he could not jump.

Lewis Carroll

I've Got a Dog

I've got a dog as thin as a rail,

He's got fleas all over his tail;

Every time his tail goes flop,

The fleas on the bottom all hop to the top.

Let Us Go to the Woods

Let us go to the woods, says this pig.

What to do there? says this pig.

To seek mamma, says this pig.

What to do with her? says this pig.

To kiss her, to kiss her, says this pig.

THERE WAS A RAT

There was a rat, for want of stairs,
Went down a rope
to say his prayers.

THIS PIG GOT IN THE BARN

This pig got in the barn,

This ate all the corn,

This said he wasn't well,

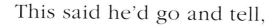

This said he'd go and tell,

And this said – weke, weke, weke,
I can't get over the barn door sill.

BEDTIME &

Hush-a-bye, baby,
On the treetop,
When the wind blows
The cradle will rock;
When the bough breaks
The cradle will fall,
Down will come baby,
Cradle, and all.

Diddle, diddle, dumpling,
My son John,
Went to bed
With his trousers on;
One shoe off,
And one shoe on,
Diddle, diddle, dumpling,
My son John.

MOONSHINE

illustrated by
Nicola Bayley

Come, let's to bed,
Says Sleepy-head;
Tarry a while, says Slow.
Put on the pan,
Says Greedy Nan,
Let's sup before we go.

Rock-a-bye, baby,
Thy cradle is green;
Father's a nobleman,
Mother's a queen;
And Betty's a lady,
And wears a gold ring;
And Johnny's a drummer,
And drums for the king.

59

INDEX OF FIRST LINES

ACKNOWLEDGEMENTS

With the exception of *No Hickory No Dickory No Dock*, all books cited are published by Walker Books.

page 8   "Out and About" is a selection of rhymes from the book of the same title.

page 12   "Monkeys on the Bed" is taken from *Tail Feathers from Mother Goose*, edited by Iona Opie.

page 14   "Michael Foreman's Mother Goose" is a selection from the book of the same title.

page 16   "Here Come the Babies" is a selection from the book of the same title.

page 20   "Clap Your Hands" is a selection from the book of the same title, edited by Sarah Hayes.

page 22   "Sugarcake Bubble" is a selection from *No Hickory No Dickory No Dock* edited by John Agard and Grace Nichols, and published in America by Candlewick Press.

page 24   "Baby Rhymes" was originally published as four books: *All Fall Down; Clap Hands; Say Goodnight; Tickle, Tickle*.

page 26   "Over the Moon" is a selection from the book of the same title.

page 32   "Two Caribbean Poems" is a selection from *A Caribbean Dozen*, edited by John Agard and Grace Nichols.

page 36   "Arnold Lobel's Mother Goose" is a selection from the book of the same title.

page 40   "Down at the Doctor's" is taken from *Spollyollydiddlytiddlyitis – The Doctor Book*.

page 41   "Messing Around" is taken from *Under the Bed – The Bedtime Book*.

page 42   "A Cup of Starshine" is a selection from the book of the same title, edited by Jill Bennett.

page 44   "Stamp Your Feet" is a selection from the book of the same title, edited by Sarah Hayes.

page 46   "I Saw Esau" is a selection from the book of the same title, edited by Iona and Peter Opie.

page 50   "Moon Frog" is taken from the book of the same title.

page 52   "If I Had a Monster" is taken from *Making Friends with Frankenstein*.

page 54   "I Never Saw a Purple Cow" is a selection from the book of the same title.

page 58   "Bedtime and Moonshine" is a selection from the book of the same title.

Throughout, where authors are not credited, they are unknown.